D1256129

Mattie's Hats
WON'T WEAR THAT!

written and illustrated by ELAINE GREENSTEIN

Alfred A. Knopf New York

http://www.randomhouse.com/

Library of Congress Cataloging-in-Publication Data: Greenstein, Elaine. Mattie's hats won't wear that! /
written by Elaine Greenstein   p.   cm. Summary: When the hats in Mattie's shop revolt against
having to wear the many exotic ornaments she attaches to them, they discover that it is special to be
different. [1. Hats—Fiction. 2. Individuality—Fiction. 3. Stores, Retail—Fiction.] I. Title.
PZ7.G8517Iae   1997   [E]—dc20   96-31233
ISBN 0-679-88349-5 (trade) ISBN 0-679-98349-X (lib. bdg.)
Manufactured in Singapore 10 9 8 7 6 5 4 3 2 1

For Brett

$\mathcal{M}$attie couldn't leave a simple hat alone.
To her, bees and a hive were the perfect topping.

With a special touch here and a slight addition there, a straw hat celebrated some of the most famous places in Paris.

A blue bowler brimmed with fruit.

A cowboy hat housed a rodeo.

All the people who walked by the shop looked twice or shook their heads or smiled.

But not many people bought hats from Mattie.

One evening, just before closing time, Harold Hirshorn, the postman, brought a package.

"Ooooh, the new ornaments!" Mattie exclaimed. "Thank you!"

Harold just shook his head.

After Mattie left the shop, a black beret peeked inside the box. Inside were the strangest hat adornments yet. Fake ice cream sundaes, a white rooster, miniature pots and pans, a motorized bear balancing on a ball, a pumpkin, and a dozen plastic elephants.

"She's nuts!" the black beret shouted. "Look at what she wants us to wear now!" He tore off the planet Saturn, which was hanging from his stem.

The other hats all agreed. "Enough of this weird stuff!"

The hats were tired of being different. They wanted to belong to someone; they wanted to be worn.

That night, the hats pulled all the ornaments off each other. Then they emptied the box onto the floor.

When Mattie came in the next morning, she thought that a burglar had been there. But nothing was gone; it was all on the floor.

Mattie was mad.

She had worked hard to make her hats.

She wouldn't let vandals get the best of her!

The black beret gave a little sigh as Mattie reattached the planet Saturn to his stem.

That night, after the shop had closed, the hats yanked all the ornaments off again. This time they left a message.

MORE STUFF!

Signed,
Your Hats

Mattie thought the vandals had been back.
Until she saw the message.

Then her shoulders slumped. No one liked
her hats—not even the hats.

She cleaned up the store, without saying a
word, and closed early.

Soon after, Eva Thistle walked by with her poodle, Clarence. They stopped by the window for a good laugh. But wait—where was the hat with the big pink pom-poms?

They left disappointed.

When Harold delivered the mail, he didn't shine his
usual big smile at the hats. He especially missed the
hat with the fish that reminded him of his vacation.

"*Tsk, tsk,*" said Prudence Underhill. "Without all the
red hearts, that hat is just dull."

After a few days, the hats began to feel lonely. It seemed as if the people who walked by looked sadder and sadder. The hats began to droop, too.

One night, the black beret complained, "Now it's worse. Before, no one bought us. Now no one even smiles at us."

Finally, Harold arrived with the mail one day and blurted out, "Mattie, I miss that hat with the fish that used to be in the window. If you could make another, I would buy it."

Mattie just sighed.

Later, Eva Thistle said, "Mattie, I wish I could surprise Clarence with the hat with the pink pom-poms for his birthday."

Mattie shook her head but smiled a little.

Then Prudence Underhill came by. "Mattie," she said, "I want a great big hat with red hearts all over it."

"I'll see what I can do" was all Mattie would say.

That night, before she closed up, Mattie took the box
of decorations down from the top of the storage closet
and placed it in the middle of the floor.

After she left, the black beret peeked inside the box.
He pulled out the planet Saturn and asked the blue
bowler to help him attach it to his stem.

Soon all the hats were trying on stuff.
Elephants paraded atop a pink hat.

A fountain sprayed the
red pillbox.

The green hat sprouted
lotus flowers.

And plastic frogs sprang
from the Panama hat.

The hats didn't quite look the way Mattie made them, but they all thought she would get the idea.

The next morning, when Mattie walked into the store, a wide smile spread across her face. "Oh, my!" she exclaimed. "You all look better than ever!"

From then on, Mattie always let the hats
help pick out their ornaments.
When the hats passed each other on the
street, they gave each other a wink. And
the black beret was happiest of all.

THE END